I0663169

The Bronze Hand

*A Mystery of Crime, Clues,
and a Supernatural Touch*

A Modern Translation

Adapted for the Contemporary Reader

Anna Katharine Green

Translated by Tim Zengerink

Table of Contents

Preface - Message to the Reader

What If You Could Help Rebuild the Greatest Library in Human History?

Thousands of years ago, the Library of Alexandria stood as the crown jewel of human achievement — a sanctuary where the collected wisdom of every known civilization was gathered, preserved, and shared freely.

And then, it was lost.

Through fire, conquest, and the slow erosion of time, humanity lost not just books — but ideas, dreams, discoveries, and stories that could have changed the world forever.

Today, the Library of Alexandria lives again — and you are invited to be a part of its restoration.

Our mission is simple yet profound:

To rebuild the greatest library the world has ever known, and to translate all timeless works into every language and dialect, so that no seeker of knowledge is ever left behind again.

By joining our movement to rebuild the modern Library of Alexandria, you become part of an unprecedented mission:

- **Unlimited Access to the Greatest Audiobooks & eBooks Ever Written:**

  Instantly explore thousands of legendary works—Plato, Shakespeare, Jane Austen, Leo Tolstoy, and countless more. All instantly available to read or listen, placing a complete literary universe at your fingertips.

- **Beautiful Paperback & Deluxe Editions at Printing Cost**

  Own any title as an elegant paperback, deluxe hardcover, or stunning collectible boxset—offered to you at true printing cost, delivered straight to your door. Build your personal Library of Alexandria, crafted for beauty, built for durability, and worthy of proud display.

- **Fresh Translations for Modern Readers—in Every Language & Dialect**

  Enjoy timeless masterpieces reimagined in clear, contemporary language—no more outdated phrases or obscure references. Alongside the original versions, we're tirelessly translating these classics into every language and dialect imaginable, ensuring accessibility and understanding across cultures and generations.

- **Join a Global Renaissance of Literature & Knowledge**

  You directly support expanding our library, publishing deluxe editions at true cost, translating works into all global languages, and bringing humanity's greatest stories to people everywhere. By joining today, you're not just preserving a legacy of masterpieces; you set in motion a powerful wave of literary accessibility.

Become a Torchbearer of Knowledge.

Join us for free now at **LibraryofAlexandria.com**

Together, we will ensure that the light of human wisdom never fades again.

With gratitude and a shared love of knowledge,

The Modern Library of Alexandria Team

Visit:

www.libraryofalexandria.com

Or scan the code below:

Introduction

A Forgotten Queen of Crime
and the Mystery Behind the Metal

Anna Katharine Green, often hailed as the "mother of the detective novel" in America, played a formative role in shaping the conventions of crime fiction long before the rise of Agatha Christie or Arthur Conan Doyle's legendary Sherlock Holmes. Born in 1846 and publishing her first novel, The Leavenworth Case, in 1878, Green introduced many tropes that have become mainstays of the genre: the legal sleuth, the clever amateur detective, the structured puzzle, and the red herring. With The Bronze Hand, a lesser-known but compelling entry in her impressive body of work, Green once again proves her uncanny ability to blend intrigue, character psychology, and symbolic menace into a tightly plotted narrative.

The Bronze Hand follows a tale of uncanny suspense, centered around a mysterious artifact that seems to exert an almost supernatural influence on the lives it touches. The titular hand, crafted from bronze and appearing at first to be an inert object, becomes the focal point of a slowly unfolding mystery involving deception, inheritance, betrayal, and the haunting grip of the past. As in much of Green's work, appearances deceive, and what initially seems inexplicable eventually finds resolution through reason—though not without a considerable detour through darkness and dread.

While Green was a pioneer of rational deduction, she was also an early master of mood, atmosphere, and dramatic irony. Her skill in crafting women characters who drive or unravel mystery narratives also distinguishes her from many of her contemporaries. In this introduction, we will examine The Bronze Hand from three essential perspectives: its historical placement within the evolution of detective fiction; its symbolic and psychological depth, particularly as it relates to gender and power; and its unique fusion of gothic and realist traditions. With this framing, the story emerges not just as a forgotten mystery, but as a foundational piece of American suspense literature.

Anna Katharine Green and the Origins of American Detective Fiction

In the late 19th century, detective fiction was still a genre in formation. While Edgar Allan Poe had written what many consider the first detective story in "The

Murders in the Rue Morgue" (1841), and Charles Dickens incorporated detection into his serialized novels, it was Anna Katharine Green who formalized the structure of the modern detective narrative. The Leavenworth Case was groundbreaking not only for its intricate plotting but for its courtroom drama, its procedural attention to legal detail, and its female protagonist—a bold move in a male-dominated genre.

By the time The Bronze Hand appeared, Green was already a well-established literary force. Her stories appealed to readers who relished logic and puzzles but also appreciated drama and moral stakes. She resisted sensationalism in favor of intellectual suspense, often placing characters in ethical as well as physical peril. Her detectives, especially the unforgettable Ebenezer Gryce, are meticulous thinkers, while her women are often agents of insight, intuition, or disruption.

In The Bronze Hand, Green plays with the conventions she helped define. The artifact at the center is not a murder weapon or a clue in the ordinary sense. It is a symbol—a talisman of unresolved tensions. The story advances not only through gathering evidence but through psychological probing, secrets disclosed through dialogue, and the gradual revelation of hidden motives. Green's writing here shows a maturity and flexibility often overlooked in discussions of early crime fiction. She bridges gothic suspense with deductive rationality, making her a precursor to both the psychological thriller and the procedural mystery.

Importantly, Green also understood her audience. She wrote for readers who were as interested in social decorum, gender roles, and domestic codes as they were in corpses and clues. In The Bronze Hand, these elements are tightly interwoven, with the mystery reflecting deeper anxieties about identity, autonomy, and the lingering influence of the past.

Symbol, Gender, and the Grip of the Past

The "bronze hand" of the title is not just a narrative device. It is a potent symbol, evoking both literal power and abstract control. Hands, in literature, are often metaphors for action, agency, and grasp. A disembodied hand, cast in an enduring metal, suggests permanence, frozen judgment, or a haunting echo of decisions made long ago. In Green's hands, so to speak, the artifact becomes a pivot for character development and dramatic revelation.

Throughout the story, women are central to the unfolding of truth. Green does not relegate her female characters to the background or make them passive observers. Instead, they are the emotional and intellectual engines of the plot. Their perceptions, intuitions, and sometimes their suppressed histories hold the keys to unraveling the mystery. In an era when women's voices were often marginalized in both literature and society, Green's work asserted the centrality of female experience to the resolution of complex moral dilemmas.

The hand itself may be interpreted as a stand-in for patriarchal legacy—a relic from the past that still exerts control over the present. Whether inherited or imposed, this legacy shapes the choices of the living. Characters must confront not only external puzzles but internal reckonings. Who am I in relation to what I've inherited? What part of my fate is mine, and what has been shaped by those long gone?

This thematic depth elevates The Bronze Hand above the level of mere entertainment. It forces readers to consider the unseen forces—societal expectations, family obligations, emotional debts—that shape human behavior. The hand that reaches out from the past is not necessarily malevolent, but it is insistent. It must be faced, its secrets understood, before the future can unfold freely.

Between the Gothic and the Rational: A Genre-Crossing Vision

While Anna Katharine Green is primarily celebrated for her influence on detective fiction, her writing frequently veers into the gothic, particularly in its use of mood, mystery, and moral ambiguity. The Bronze Hand demonstrates this hybrid sensibility in full force. The story opens with an atmosphere of unease: an artifact charged with mystery, strange occurrences that defy immediate explanation, and characters driven by forces they do not entirely comprehend.

Yet Green always returns to clarity. She does not allow the supernatural to take over. Her stories may flirt with the uncanny, but they remain rooted in psychological realism and empirical reasoning. In this, she resembles authors like Wilkie Collins, who used gothic elements to enrich his social and criminal investigations. The Bronze Hand belongs to this lineage—a gothic-inflected mystery that deepens character and plot through symbolic suggestion rather than spectral interference.

This balance between gothic shadow and rational light is part of Green's enduring genius. She offers her readers the pleasures of suspense, emotional intensity, and eerie imagery, without abandoning the fundamental principle that truth can be found, justice can be served, and mysteries are solvable through intellect and insight. Her world is not random; it is haunted by meaning.

As you read this modern translation of The Bronze Hand, pay attention not only to the unfolding plot, but to the subtler currents beneath it. Notice how the past insists on recognition. Notice how women speak when silence is expected. And notice how a symbol as simple as a sculpted hand can hold within it the weight of memory, power, and the enduring search for truth.

In rediscovering Anna Katharine Green, we are not merely looking back. We are uncovering the origins of so much that we now take for granted in modern mystery fiction. And in The Bronze Hand, her genius remains firmly, and thrillingly, intact.

I.

The Fascinating Unknown

She lived on the ground floor of the house we both stayed in, and I lived right above her. The only times I ever saw her were when she leaned out to shut her shutters at night or open them in the morning. But even those short glimpses of her reddish-brown hair left a strong impression on me. Her pale face, framed by that warm color, became my idea of beauty and mystery.

She was a mystery to me.

I'm busy now, but back then, I had more free time than I knew what to do with. It was during a tense period—right after John Brown's raid on Harper's Ferry. Abraham Lincoln had just been elected president. In Baltimore, where all of this happened, groups were quietly forming to work against the North. People who felt deeply wronged were planning bold, secret actions. These plans were big, far-reaching, and hidden.

During that time, everyone was on edge. People who spoke too openly weren't trusted, and those who stayed quiet were also suspicious. It was hard for thoughtful people to relax, especially with nothing to keep them busy. Maybe that's why I spent so much time at my window.

One night, I was sitting there when I suddenly heard a sharp cry from the room below. It was her voice—one I'd been waiting to hear. Any sound from her would've caught my attention, but this one was filled with emotion. I had to see what happened.

I leaned out and looked down. I saw one of her shutters swinging in the wind and a man running off around the corner. Her window, like mine, was wide open, and light was pouring out.

As I kept watching, she leaned out too. She looked both ways with clear fear on her face. I heard her whisper something, her voice shaking. I couldn't stay silent.

"Excuse me, miss—was that man who just ran off bothering you?" I called down.

She gasped and looked up at me. I'll never forget that face—so striking, so full of emotion. She met my eyes and said:

"You saw him? You saw the man? Oh, please, can I speak to you for just a moment?"

I almost jumped straight down to help her but quickly reminded myself I wasn't a storybook hero.

Instead, I told her I'd be there in a second and took the stairs down as fast as I could.

It wasn't far, but my heart was pounding by the time I reached the bottom. I had never imagined being invited into her world. But now, here I was.

Her door was already open. Before she noticed me, I saw her staring at her right hand with a look of horror. She looked strong and scared all at once—almost like someone from a dream.

She turned suddenly and waved me closer.

"Oh!" she said. "You're the man from upstairs— the one who saw someone running! Do you think you could recognize him again?"

"I don't think so," I said honestly. "He was gone in a second. I barely saw anything."

"Oh," she moaned, wringing her hands. Then she straightened up and looked me right in the eyes.

"I need a friend," she said quietly, "but I'm surrounded by strangers."

I stepped toward her. I didn't feel like a stranger at all—but how could I show her that?

"If there's anything I can do…" I began.

She studied my face for a long moment.

"I've seen you before," she said simply. "You seem like someone I can trust. But I need more than kindness. I need someone brave, loyal, careful—and willing to put me first. That's a lot to ask of someone I barely know."

It felt like she was gently pushing me away. She turned her back, then looked over her shoulder and said:

"I'm overwhelmed. Please just let me be. There's nothing you can do."

If she had seemed fake or dramatic, I might have left. But her pain felt real—too real to ignore. I couldn't stop myself. I said, like the passionate 21-year-old I was:

"I'll risk my life for you. I don't know why, and I don't care. All I know is, you won't find anyone more ready to help."

She gave me a soft, surprised smile—almost touched by what I said. Then she shook her head, like she was trying to stay grounded. It looked like she was about to turn me down again. But then, just as suddenly, she changed her mind. She accepted my offer with such urgency that it made me even more determined to help her.

"I can read people," she said. "And I think you'll do what I can't. But first—do you have a mother?"

I told her no. I didn't have many close family members.

"Good," she said quietly, almost to herself. Then she looked back at me. "Do you have a girlfriend?"

I must've turned bright red, because she pulled back a little. But I quickly reassured her. Whatever I said seemed to comfort her, because her next words showed she was ready to trust me.

"I lost a ring," she said quickly, her voice low and urgent. "It was pulled from my finger when I reached out to close the shutters. Someone was waiting— someone who knew exactly when I shut my window every night. The ring means more than you can imagine. It's more than just a piece of jewelry. If someone brings it back to me, straight from the person who stole it, I'd be grateful for the rest of my life. Will you try? I can't go to the police with this."

Her request was so unexpected that it stopped me cold—and stirred up a bit of jealousy too.

"But isn't this exactly the kind of thing the police handle?" I asked, imagining how foolish I'd look chasing down what seemed like a simple keepsake.

"I know it probably seems that way," she replied, clearly picking up on my doubt. "But what officer would spend time searching for something worth less than five dollars?"

"So it's just a memento?" I asked, my voice giving away how I felt.

"Yes, just a memento," she said. "But not from someone I loved. Still, even though it's worthless in money, I'd give up everything I own for it tonight—almost even my soul. I can't explain more than that. Will you try to get it back?"

Hearing that it wasn't from a lover brought me back to my senses. The mystery and strength in her words, her beauty, and the energy of her presence took over completely. I stopped thinking logically and said with all the emotion I felt:

"I'll get the ring back for you. Just tell me where to go and who I'm up against. If it can be done, I'll bring it to you by morning."

"Oh!" she said, shaking her head. "You think this will be easy. But it won't be. I don't even know who took it—I only know where it's going. And if it reaches that place, then all hope is lost."

"No love token," I whispered, "but it still means everything to you?"

"More than just everything," she replied.

Then, without warning, she turned and shut the door behind me. The loud click made me realize I had stepped into something serious—something far bigger than I had expected. It had to be a political secret of some kind, something dangerous. But I didn't care. My expression must've shown her that, because she stepped closer and said:

"Listen. I'm keeping a secret. I'm here, in this house, in this city, for a reason. The secret isn't mine, so I can't share it. And I can't tell you what my mission is. That means if you help me, you'll be walking into real danger—completely blind. But I can tell you this: you'll be on the right side. You'll be fighting against something wrong. Even if you fail, you'll have risked your life for a cause that matters. Do you understand, Mr...?"

"Abbott," I said with a nod.

She took that as my answer. "So you don't back down," she said softly. "Not even when I tell you that you can't tell anyone about this—not a word, even if things get bad."

"If I was the kind of man to back down," I said with a smile, "I wouldn't be standing here now."

She raised her hand, serious now.

"Swear it," she said. "Swear that from the moment you leave this room until you come back, you won't say a single word about me, your mission, or even the promise I'm making you swear right now."

This is serious, I thought. But still, under her spell, I gave her my word—and I didn't regret it.

"No more delay," she said firmly. "There's an office in a large building on ——— Street. The name on the door is Dr. Merriam. Here—" she handed me a card, "—so you don't forget."

"He sees patients between ten and twelve in the morning. During those hours, anyone can go in. But to avoid suspicion, you'll need a reason. Can you come up with a medical problem?"

"I don't think so," I said. "But maybe I could fake one."

"No," she warned. "Dr. Merriam is smart. He'd see through any lie."

"I have a sick friend," I said, thinking quickly. "His case is strange. I could easily get the doctor's attention with it."

"Perfect," she said. "Talk to him about your friend. But while you wait, keep an eye on a large box on a side table. Don't stare at it, but don't lose sight of it either—

not from the moment you walk in until you leave at noon. If you get a minute alone (and you might, as long as you don't rush the doctor), open the box with this key—" she handed it to me—"and check what's inside. No one will stop you. You won't be the only one with access to that box."

"But—" I began.

"You'll find something there," she whispered. "It's a bronze hand resting on a fancy cushion. On the fingers of that hand, there should be rings made of steel—each one uniquely made. If there's a ring on the middle finger, then it's over for me. My cause is lost, and I'll just have to wait for the worst." Her face turned pale. "But if the ring isn't there yet, then someone— though I don't know who—will try to put one on it tomorrow before noon. That ring will be mine—the one that was just stolen from me. Your job is to stop that box from being opened so they can't do it. But you must do it quietly. No calling attention, no police, no arrests or investigations. That would ruin everything. Even just one day of delay could make a huge difference. It would give me time to think, maybe even to act. Does it sound impossible? Am I asking too much from someone like you?"

"It doesn't sound easy," I admitted. "But I'm willing to try. What kind of danger am I facing? And if I do see the ring on the finger, why can't I just take it off and bring it back to you?"

"Because," she said, answering the second question first, "once the ring slides over the final joint, it becomes part of a mechanism. You won't be able to pull it off. As for the danger... it's hidden. It's part of the secret I told you I couldn't share. But if you're smart, brave, and careful, you might get through it. Just know this: if someone accuses you of interfering, they have to prove it. That rule has never been broken."

I was stunned by how mysterious and dangerous this all sounded. For a moment, I thought about backing out. But I was only twenty-one, with too much time on my hands—and I was already too drawn in by my feelings for her to say no. The excitement was too strong. I laughed to shake off some nerves, stood up tall, and said something brave—I don't even know if she heard it. Then I asked something about the doctor, which made her perk up.

"The doctor," she said, "might know what the box is really about—or he might not. My advice: treat him like he's just a doctor. Anyone using that key"—she pointed to the one she had given me—"must be careful and quiet. I wish I could go myself, but I'd be too emotional. And they know what I look like. That's the only reason the ring was stolen from me."

"I'll go for you," I promised. "Anything else I need to know?"

"No," she said. "In a case like this, no amount of instructions will help. You'll have to decide what to do in the moment. Just know I'll be thinking of you the whole time. Goodnight, sir. I hope it's not goodbye."

"One last thing," I said, getting ready to leave. "Would you mind telling me your name?"

"I'm Miss Calhoun," she said with a graceful nod.

And that was the beginning of my strange and dangerous adventure with the bronze hand.

II.

The Quaker-Like Girl, the Pale Girl, and the Man with A Bristling Mustache

The building my new friend told me about was already familiar. It was the kind of place where almost every office stayed empty all year. The few people who did rent space there rarely paid on time and barely cared about their own work, let alone anyone else's. The public avoided it completely, and the tenants didn't try to make it any better. Even though it stood at a busy city corner, it felt as empty and forgotten as an old ruin. People may have looked out of its dirty windows now and then, but no one walking by ever gave it a second thought. No one even bothered to feel sorry for it. Its walls were dark with grime, and the staircases and hallways were thick with undisturbed dust.

If someone had been looking for a secret, hidden place, this building would've been perfect. As I got closer to the door with the doctor's name on it, I found myself walking quietly, like I didn't want to be heard. I wasn't sure if it was from nervousness or fear, but I definitely felt on edge.

I had planned to arrive exactly at ten o'clock and was sure I'd be the first one there. I reached for the doorknob, thinking I could slip in without anyone noticing. But as soon as I turned it, it let out a loud, rusty squeal that made me cringe and echoed down the hallway. Goosebumps ran over me as I pushed the door open and stepped into the doctor's waiting room.

To my surprise, it wasn't empty. Around a dozen people, both men and women, sat in chairs lined up along the walls. They all had that distracted look people get when waiting to see the doctor. One woman was trying to act casual by using her pretty shoe to push at a nail sticking out of the floor. Maybe she was trying to be playful, and on a normal day I might've found it charming—but not here. Another man sat staring at a spider web, almost like he was counting the flies caught in it. That fit the gloomy mood of the room better.

I believed the ring I was looking for was in someone's possession there, so I carefully studied each person as best I could. Two stood out. One was a young man with sharp features and very bright blue eyes that kept darting around the room. His constant glancing made the rest of us feel anxious too. Why wasn't he as gloomy as the others?

The second was the girl with the pretty shoe. She stood out not just because of her beauty, but also because of her plain, modest clothing. She was restless too—her foot had stopped moving, but now her hands wouldn't stay still. She kept gripping them in her lap, then running one hand over and around a small but expensive leather bag hanging by her side. I stared at it and thought, She has the ring. I sat down in the seat beside her.

I also couldn't help but notice the box. It sat on a simple wooden table directly across from the door I had entered. About a foot wide, it was the only nice-looking thing in the room. With little else to look at, most of us kept glancing at it, although hardly anyone seemed truly interested. That gave me hope, and I was about to focus all my attention on the two suspects when one of them—the girl—suddenly stood up and left the room.

I wasn't expecting that. Did I make her nervous by watching her? Or had she figured out why I was there? Unsure, I looked at the man I thought might be working with her. His face showed nothing. While I was trying to figure it out, I noticed another woman sitting next to where the girl had been. She looked pale and very sick, like she might faint at any moment. Her head hung low, and she looked like she barely had the strength to sit upright. But when the door to the doctor's office opened and he stepped out, clearly ready for the next patient, she didn't move. Instead, she nudged another woman forward who didn't seem nearly as sick. I had to remind myself that this wasn't a dream—everything I was seeing was real.

Curious about her strange behavior, I kept watching the pale girl. I actually started to feel sorry for her. But then, something happened that made me remember exactly why I was there. Without warning, she jumped up like someone in pain and staggered over to the table with the box. She looked like she was about to collapse as she leaned on it, struggling to breathe.

The good-looking man nearby made a small noise, like a grunt, but he didn't move to help her. Neither did the older woman with a skin condition sitting close by, even though she seemed like she wanted to. I was the only one who stood. I couldn't let someone touch that box without getting involved. Trying to hide what I was really thinking, I walked over to the girl and said politely:

"You look really sick. Do you want me to get the doctor?"

She was holding onto the table to keep herself steady, her head hanging low, moving side to side as if in pain.

"Thank you," she said without turning to me. "I'll wait. I'd rather wait."

Just then, the doctor's door opened again.

"There he is now," I said.

"I'll wait," she repeated. "Let the others go first."

Now I was sure something else was going on—she wasn't just sick. I stepped back and wondered whether she had always had the ring, or if the girl who left had passed it to her. In the meantime, another patient had gone into the doctor's room.

Time passed slowly. The man with the darting eyes started to get more fidgety. Was she guarding the box, and he wanted to open it? As that idea came to me, I took a closer look at her. She definitely wasn't just using her hand for support—she was doing something else. Then I heard a soft click. She was unlocking the box.

Trying not to look alarmed, I kept calm and pretended to be busy. I pulled out a small notebook and began to write in it. Meanwhile, the doctor finished with another patient and called for the next one. To my surprise, the restless young man stood up and went in.

That cleared him in my mind—he must not have been after the box after all.

The doctor's meeting with the man took a while. During that time, the young woman sitting by the window barely moved. When the fourth person left, she turned and gave a quick look at me and the other person in the room.

I understood right away—she was waiting for the chance to be alone so she could open that strange box. She wasn't really sick at all.

In fact, her cheeks had some color, and the way she trembled was clearly from excitement or nerves, not from pain. My sympathy quickly turned into frustration, and I told myself I wouldn't go easy on her if we ended up fighting over that box.

The only other person in the room was an old man who seemed clueless. He'd come in after the rest of us. When the doctor came back, I motioned for the old man to go next, and he eagerly followed the doctor out, leaving just me and the girl behind.

Right away, I stood up, stretched a little, and yawned as if I were bored.

"This is taking forever," I said out loud and slowly wandered toward the hallway door.

The girl near the box couldn't hide her impatience. She gave me another quick glance, but I pretended not to notice. I pulled out my watch, checked the time, slipped it back in my pocket, and walked into the hallway. As soon as I shut the door behind me, I heard a soft creak.

I rushed back in and caught her off guard. She was leaning over the open box.

"Oh no, miss," I said, hurrying toward her and pretending to be concerned. "You don't look well at all. If you're feeling faint, lean on me—I'll help you sit down."

She spun around, clearly angry, but when she saw my face, she tried to act calm. I wasn't fooled. I stepped closer and peeked into the box before she had a chance to shut it.

What I saw didn't surprise me, but it was still fascinating. Inside was a bronze hand, beautifully made, resting on a soft cushion. It had rings on every finger— except the middle one. That was good. It meant Miss Calhoun hadn't succeeded in doing whatever she was planning yet.

Now feeling in control again, I looked into the box with a curious but relaxed expression. I was even surprised at how calmly I was handling it.

"That's a strange thing to find in a doctor's office," I said. "Beautiful, though. A really interesting piece of art. But there's nothing scary about it. You shouldn't let something like that upset you." And before she could stop me, I quickly closed the lid with a firm snap.

She stepped back, clearly upset, and quickly hid her hands behind her.

"You're being very pushy," she said sharply. But when she saw the friendly smile I gave her, she hesitated. Then, falling back into her earlier act, she started moaning softly and dropped into the nearest chair. A second later, she jumped back up with a dramatic cry: "Oh, I feel awful! I shouldn't have come here alone!" Then, moving much faster than someone sick should be able to, she rushed into the hall and slammed the door behind her.

I was surprised at how easily I had won. At first, I just stood there, proud of myself, and tried to open the box again. But it was locked tight. I was just deciding whether to return to my seat when the hall door opened and a new man came in.

He was short and stocky, with a thick black mustache. The moment I saw him, I knew he was interested in both the box and me. I didn't let it show, but I got ready for something more serious than the scene I had just handled.

Trying to mimic the girl's earlier behavior, I leaned my elbow on the box and stared out the window. As I did, I heard some movement in the next room and knew the doctor was about to call for another patient.

I had a problem. If the doctor picked me next, I would have to leave, and the man who just entered was clearly here to open the box. He wasn't going to leave while I was gone. So how could I go in and still protect the box?

There was only one solution, and I had come prepared. While standing close to the box, I pressed a small piece of wax—something I'd been warming in my hand—into the keyhole. Then, I placed my hat carefully on top of the box, making sure to remember exactly how it lined up with the patterns and shapes carved into the lid. That way, if the hat was moved while I was gone, I'd know.

By then, the doctor had come to the door. Feeling confident in my plan, I followed him calmly into the office.

Dr. Merriam, who I hadn't described until now, was tall and solidly built. He was bald, had kind eyes, and seemed friendly, but he didn't pay much attention to his clothes or appearance. When I looked into his eyes and returned his warm greeting, I had a strong feeling that he wasn't as interested in the box as his role as its guardian might suggest. And as I started talking to him about my friend's condition, I noticed something right away—he was deeply fascinated by unusual medical cases. The moment I mentioned my friend's symptoms, his whole focus shifted. Whatever connection he had to the box, it clearly didn't matter as much to him as the chance to explore a strange new illness.

So I shared all the details he asked for and was able to get some truly helpful advice, which I genuinely appreciated.

When we were finished, I told him I was leaving, but instead of using the regular exit, I said I had forgotten my hat in the waiting room and turned back the way I had come. But I wasn't expecting what I saw next.

There was still only one person in the room with the box—but it wasn't the mustached man with the serious expression I thought I'd find. Instead, it was the calm-looking young woman I had suspected earlier. Even though she was sitting far from the box, one glance at her flushed cheeks and shaking hands told me she had just been over there.

I went straight to the box and noticed my hat had been moved. But the biggest clue was on the floor—a hairpin with a bit of wax stuck to the end of it. That proved everything. The man must have figured out why his key wouldn't turn and had brought the girl in to help. She had been waiting outside in the hall, and she had tried to remove the wax. Thankfully, I had come in at just the right moment to stop her.

Feeling proud that my plan had worked and confident that the box was safe for the day—it was almost noon now—I exchanged a few more words with the doctor, who had followed me into the room. Then I got ready to leave. But the girl was quicker than me.

She said something about having an urgent appointment and not being able to see the doctor after all. Then she rushed out of the room and down the hallway. The doctor looked confused but just shrugged it off.

I wanted badly to follow her, but I paused at the doorway. That's when I saw something small under the chair she had been sitting in. It was the little leather bag I had seen her wearing earlier.

I grabbed it and told the doctor I'd catch up to her and return it. Honestly, I was glad to have a reason to follow her without seeming suspicious. I hurried downstairs and managed to reach the sidewalk just in time to see her turning the corner. I was only a few steps behind her—and I made sure to keep it that way.

III.

Madame

I wasn't following the girl just to return her bag—I wanted to know where she was going. I was sure that the three people who had shown interest in the box weren't the ones truly in charge. I needed to find out who really was behind it all. So I kept walking after her.

She led me into a sketchy part of the city. As the crowds thinned and we were the only two people on the block, I got nervous she might turn around and spot me before reaching her destination. But she didn't seem to suspect anything. She calmly walked up the steps of a building in the middle of the block and went through an open door. A brass plate on the door had one word written in big black letters:

"MADAME."

That was strange. I didn't want to walk into a place like that without knowing who "Madame" was or what went on inside. I looked around for someone who could tell me. Across the street, I saw an upholstery shop. A man stood in the doorway, and he looked friendly enough. I went over and pointed at the house the girl had entered.

"What kind of place is that?" I asked.

He smiled.

"Go and see," he said. "The door's open. And don't worry—they don't charge anything," he added quickly, maybe thinking I looked unsure. "I've been in there once myself. Everyone just sits around and she talks— if she feels like it. It's all nonsense, though. Doesn't really mean anything."

"But is it dangerous?" I asked. "Is it a safe place?"

"Oh, safe enough. Never heard of anything bad happening. Real ladies go there—though they wear veils. I've seen two fancy carriages waiting out front at the same time. They're fools, sure, but probably honest."

That was all I needed to hear. I crossed the street again and walked into the open house. Inside was a large hallway. A quiet Black woman led me into a long, dimly lit room that felt like stepping out of the noisy city into some kind of strange, sacred place.

The room gave off a mysterious feeling. The light was soft and low, like in a place of worship. I could smell burning incense in the air. Men and women were seated quietly on low benches along the walls. In the center of the room, on a raised platform in front of a black velvet curtain, sat a woman dressed in colorful fabrics, shining with gold, her body wrapped tightly like a statue. She reminded me of a Hindu idol—one of those you see in books about temples. Her face, partly visible in the low light, looked as lifeless as carved wood. Her expression wasn't exactly ugly, but it had something chilling about it. Cold, harsh, and without emotion— yet strangely threatening. Anyone who came there seeking answers would have been deeply affected by just looking at her.

I told myself I wouldn't fall for it. But within two minutes of looking at her, I felt myself forgetting why I'd come. I sat down like everyone else, waiting for something I couldn't even name.

I don't know how long I sat there, completely still. It felt like I was under a spell. Then, suddenly, I snapped out of it. I'm not sure how or why. No one else in the room had moved. I forced myself to stay alert, afraid I'd get drawn back into that daze. Thankfully, I fully remembered what I was there for.

Now fully awake, I looked around to see if others were reacting the same way. That's when I caught the eye of the young woman whose bag I still held. She had noticed me. She wasn't hypnotized. She recognized me.

I held out her bag. She glanced nervously at Madame, then grabbed the bag from me. I tried to say something—to explain—but I didn't get the chance.

Just then, a voice echoed through the room.

From the way everyone reacted, I knew it could only be Madame speaking. Her voice didn't sound human at first—more like a soft, musical hum from far away. It reminded me of the sound snake charmers use in stories to summon cobras. Everyone leaned in to listen. I did too. All the silence, all the build-up—it had to lead to something important. What was she going to say?

Slowly, her sounds became words. The room was so quiet it felt like no one dared to breathe. People wanted to hear something personal—some kind of warning or prediction. With so much uncertainty in the world, they were desperate to know what the future held.

Finally, in a low, steady voice, she said:

"Doom! Doom! For the one who betrayed—his time is up, the bell is tolling. Hear this, all of you who feel powerless—let it make you stronger. And you, who think you're powerful—be afraid. The bell won't just toll for him. It will toll for every one of you... if the decision of the joined rings is made—"

Just then, I saw the velvet curtain behind her move slightly. Maybe no one else noticed, but I did. So when a very pale hand reached out from behind the curtain and gently touched Madame's right temple, I wasn't exactly surprised. What did surprise me, though, was realizing something important—that this strange woman, who seemed totally disconnected from politics or real-world issues, was in fact somehow involved in the very conspiracy I was trying to stop.

But how involved was she? Was she the leader? Or just a puppet, controlled by someone more powerful—maybe the owner of that pale hand?

I had no way of knowing yet.

The hand pulled back, and Madame looked like she had fallen back into a trance. After a moment, she said softly:

"I have spoken."

The silence that followed gave me time to think. What had she just said? She warned the powerful to be afraid. She had spoken of death for "the betrayer." Was it just creepy nonsense? A psychic vision? Or a direct threat?

I leaned toward the last option. And here's why: for the past few weeks, there had been a disturbing rise in sudden deaths—some even called them murders. I remembered the reports from cities like St. Louis, Boston, New Orleans, New York, and even here in Baltimore. All the victims had some connection to the political unrest happening at the time.

As all this came together in my mind, I couldn't help but think Madame's strange speech might confirm the worst fears Miss Calhoun had hinted at.

I'd been so lost in my own thoughts that I worried I might've drawn unwanted attention. I glanced to one side nervously—then I heard someone speak from the other direction:

"She's never been wrong. What she says always happens. Someone important is going to die."

Those dark words broke the heavy silence in the room. I turned to see who had spoken and locked eyes with a man whose features chilled me—a sloped forehead, a weak chin, and a mouth so wide and cruel that he looked like someone dangerously unstable, the kind of person who could be easily used by others for terrible things.

Whoever this man was, he clearly understood the meaning of Madame's prediction. And he looked like the type who could actually help make it come true.

I quickly turned my gaze away from his disturbing face and looked back at Madame. She hadn't moved, but either the light in the room had changed or my eyes had adjusted, because now I could see her more clearly. Her eyelids were open, and her eyes were staring directly at me. It made me uneasy. There was something cold, maybe even hateful, in her look. I began to regret ever stepping into that place.

Trying to calm myself, I let my eyes drift down to her hands, which were folded across her chest. But that didn't help. In the clearer light, I noticed they were shiny and dark, covered in rings—and they looked eerily like the bronze hand I had seen earlier in Dr. Merriam's office.

I'd never thought of myself as easily scared, but in that moment, a creeping fear of Madame took hold of me. And I wasn't the only one. The girl who had led me there also seemed visibly shaken, and that only made me more anxious.

The room was silent again. The kind of silence that presses down on you. I refused to give in to the fear, even though I could feel it in my chest. I let my eyes wander again, looking for anything to break the stillness. That's when I noticed something moving—a man's foot, just barely sticking out from behind the curtain where I'd seen the pale hand earlier. It was swinging restlessly up and down, like he was impatient. That normal, human motion felt completely out of place in a room so full of tension and mystery. Who was this man, calmly fidgeting while everyone else was under a spell? Was he watching over Madame? Was he in charge?

I couldn't tell, and the curtain kept its secrets. So I looked back at Madame's face.

Her expression had changed. Her eyes were no longer on me—they stared into empty space, like she was seeing something terrible only she could understand. Her lips, once tightly closed, parted. She began to speak.

"'Vengeance is mine. I will repay,' says the Lord."

The voice was no longer soft. It cracked and rang with anger. The man's foot behind the curtain stopped moving.

Madame continued:

"Through pain, sorrow, blood, and death, victory will come. A life for a life. Pain for pain. Hate for hate!"

Then, just like before, the small white hand appeared from behind the curtain and touched her forehead. But this time, it didn't calm her. Instead, it seemed to fuel her, pushing her into another outburst.

She spoke faster, more wildly, like she wasn't just seeing something, but reliving it—some memory so powerful it had taken over her completely.

"I see a child—a girl. She's young. She's beautiful. Many men love her, but she only loves one. He's from the North. She's from the South. He's cold like the snow. She burns like the sun. The fire can't melt the ice. The ice kills the fire. Tragedy! Tragedy!"

Now the left hand came through the curtain too, touching her left temple. But it didn't help. Her words poured out even faster, tangled up in rage.

"She becomes a woman. She has a child. The man demands the child. She refuses. He curses the child— he curses her—but she holds the baby close, even as he beats her arms black and blue. Then he curses her homeland—the land that gave her that love. And hearing that, she stands and curses him and all that he stands for—with a vow so fierce that even God will hear it from His throne of judgment."

Her voice shook the room.

"The child dies between them—its small, lifeless body forever blocking the path of forgiveness. There will be no peace. Only grief. Only sorrow."

And just like that, as suddenly as she had erupted, she went still. Her face froze again. Her eyes stayed wide and blank, but a cold, cruel smile crept across her lips— as if, by speaking those final words, she had seen a future full of violence and blood, and it satisfied something dark inside her.

It was disturbing—awful, even—but no one else seemed to feel the same way I did. To the others, it was just a glimpse into someone's suffering. But for me, it felt like I was watching the root of something dark— something that had already caused pain and would cause even more, and this woman had no pity for any of it. I felt powerless to stop it.

It was also clear that Madame hadn't meant for her followers to hear her wild outburst. Just then, the man with the pale hands who had tried to calm her stepped out from behind the curtain. I recognized him right away—he was the same man with the sharp mustache whose plan I had messed up earlier by jamming the keyhole of the box with wax.

That told me everything. This was a setup. A trick, I thought. But a dangerous one. The ring—whose capture was now clearly tied to someone's life—was in one of their hands. Was it with this man? With Madame? Or with the quiet girl sitting nearby?

I had no way of knowing yet, but I had to find out.

While I watched the man, I noticed something interesting. He looked calm on the outside, but I saw his hand clench slightly, like he was hiding nerves. He spoke carefully, but quickly, like he wanted to finish and get out before showing any weakness.

"Madame will wake soon," he said. "She won't speak again today. If you wish, you may walk past and kiss the edge of her robe. But she's still far from this world—too far to hear or answer anyone. Please remain silent."

So it was all an act. Or maybe it was a tactic to get me closer—or just to keep the other believers convinced. Either way, I didn't care. What mattered was getting a good look at Madame, up close, without the distance or mystery between us.

I joined the slow line of people walking toward her. I wasn't going to kiss her robe, but I wanted to see her face clearly—and especially, her hands.

As I approached, all my attention shifted to her right hand. On the middle finger, I saw it: the ring—the very one the young woman had described. If her description was right, this was it.

Seeing it there, I was certain. I can take it, I told myself. Confidence surged through me.

I acted calm and respectful, gave a slight bow, and walked past her like everyone else. But my mind was racing. I had made a decision—I would come back for it.

When I reached the door, I waited until everyone else had exited. Then I turned around and walked back to Madame.

She was alone. The man who had been watching her had left the room. This was better than I had hoped for.

With firm steps, I walked up to her again and stood directly in front of her. She didn't react, but I didn't let that stop me. I stared her down, focusing all my strength, then spoke clearly and firmly, like someone in control.

"Madame," I said, "the man you've been waiting for is here. Give me the ring. Stop trusting messengers who are weak or false."

The way she reacted was shocking. She suddenly came alive, lifting her heavy eyelids and locking eyes with me. Her stare was just as intense as mine, but I didn't look away. I held her gaze with quiet confidence. I saw something shift in her—just slightly, but it was there. Her expression, once like stone, flickered with the first hint of emotion.

"You?" she said softly, almost sweetly. "Why should I trust you more than the others?"

"I'm the one you were expecting," I replied, pushing forward while her resistance was fading. "Haven't you felt it? Didn't you know I'd come? The one who leads was meant to stand before you today."

She shook slightly. Her arms loosened just a little.

"I've had dreams," she whispered. "But I've been warned not to trust dreams. If you are who you say you are, show me a sign—something real. What proof do you have?"

I hesitated for a second, but I couldn't back down now. "This," I said, pulling the key from my pocket—the one the young woman had given me.

She moved forward slightly and touched the key with her finger. Then she looked at me again.

"Others have keys too," she said. "But they can't open the lock. What makes you any different?"

"You know I am," I said firmly. "You know I can do what they couldn't. Give me the ring."

My words had power. She trembled, gave me one final look, and then slowly began to slide the ring from her finger. She held it in her hand and started to pass it to me.

But just before it reached me, a voice broke through the silence.

"Madame, be careful," it said. "That's the man who plugged the lock and ruined my efforts at the doctor's office."

She pulled her hand back. But I was too fast—I grabbed the ring before she could put it back on.

Holding it tightly, I turned to the speaker with a calm, cold look.

"Don't bother arguing with me," I said. "I stopped you because I saw how reckless and unworthy you were. This job needs someone everyone can count on. Now that I have the ring, this will all end soon. Madame, you need to choose your allies more wisely. Tomorrow, this ring will be right where it belongs."

I bowed like before and headed to the door. No one tried to stop me. I felt a surge of pride and relief—my boldness had worked.

But just as I stepped out of the room, I heard a laugh behind me. It was sharp, loud, and mocking. I froze. Something was wrong.

I looked down at the ring in my hand.

It wasn't the special steel ring meant for the device in the doctor's office—it was just an ordinary gold ring.

She had tricked me. She had given me the wrong one. And by taking it, I had revealed that I wasn't who I claimed to be.

There was nothing left to do but leave—defeated and humiliated.

IV.

Checkmate

It was disturbing—awful, even—but no one else seemed to feel the same way I did. To the others, it was just a glimpse into someone's suffering. But for me, it felt like I was watching the root of something dark— something that had already caused pain and would cause even more, and this woman had no pity for any of it. I felt powerless to stop it.

It was also clear that Madame hadn't meant for her followers to hear her wild outburst. Just then, the man with the pale hands who had tried to calm her stepped out from behind the curtain. I recognized him right away—he was the same man with the sharp mustache whose plan I had messed up earlier by jamming the keyhole of the box with wax.

That told me everything. This was a setup. A trick, I thought. But a dangerous one. The ring—whose capture was now clearly tied to someone's life—was in one of their hands. Was it with this man? With Madame? Or with the quiet girl sitting nearby?

I had no way of knowing yet, but I had to find out.

While I watched the man, I noticed something interesting. He looked calm on the outside, but I saw his hand clench slightly, like he was hiding nerves. He spoke carefully, but quickly, like he wanted to finish and get out before showing any weakness.

"Madame will wake soon," he said. "She won't speak again today. If you wish, you may walk past and kiss the edge of her robe. But she's still far from this world—too far to hear or answer anyone. Please remain silent."

So it was all an act. Or maybe it was a tactic to get me closer—or just to keep the other believers convinced. Either way, I didn't care. What mattered was getting a good look at Madame, up close, without the distance or mystery between us.

I joined the slow line of people walking toward her. I wasn't going to kiss her robe, but I wanted to see her face clearly—and especially, her hands.

As I approached, all my attention shifted to her right hand. On the middle finger, I saw it: the ring—the very one the young woman had described. If her description was right, this was it.

Seeing it there, I was certain. I can take it, I told myself. Confidence surged through me.

I acted calm and respectful, gave a slight bow, and walked past her like everyone else. But my mind was racing. I had made a decision—I would come back for it.

When I reached the door, I waited until everyone else had exited. Then I turned around and walked back to Madame.

She was alone. The man who had been watching her had left the room. This was better than I had hoped for.

With firm steps, I walked up to her again and stood directly in front of her. She didn't react, but I didn't let that stop me. I stared her down, focusing all my strength, then spoke clearly and firmly, like someone in control.

"Madame," I said, "the man you've been waiting for is here. Give me the ring. Stop trusting messengers who are weak or false."

The way she reacted was shocking. She suddenly came alive, lifting her heavy eyelids and locking eyes with me. Her stare was just as intense as mine, but I didn't look away. I held her gaze with quiet confidence. I saw something shift in her—just slightly, but it was there. Her expression, once like stone, flickered with the first hint of emotion.

"You?" she said softly, almost sweetly. "Why should I trust you more than the others?"

"I'm the one you were expecting," I replied, pushing forward while her resistance was fading. "Haven't you felt it? Didn't you know I'd come? The one who leads was meant to stand before you today."

She shook slightly. Her arms loosened just a little.

"I've had dreams," she whispered. "But I've been warned not to trust dreams. If you are who you say you are, show me a sign—something real. What proof do you have?"

I hesitated for a second, but I couldn't back down now. "This," I said, pulling the key from my pocket— the one the young woman had given me.

She moved forward slightly and touched the key with her finger. Then she looked at me again.

"Others have keys too," she said. "But they can't open the lock. What makes you any different?"

"You know I am," I said firmly. "You know I can do what they couldn't. Give me the ring."

My words had power. She trembled, gave me one final look, and then slowly began to slide the ring from her finger. She held it in her hand and started to pass it to me.

But just before it reached me, a voice broke through the silence.

"Madame, be careful," it said. "That's the man who plugged the lock and ruined my efforts at the doctor's office."

She pulled her hand back. But I was too fast—I grabbed the ring before she could put it back on.

Holding it tightly, I turned to the speaker with a calm, cold look.

"Don't bother arguing with me," I said. "I stopped you because I saw how reckless and unworthy you were. This job needs someone everyone can count on. Now that I have the ring, this will all end soon. Madame, you need to choose your allies more wisely. Tomorrow, this ring will be right where it belongs."

I bowed like before and headed to the door. No one tried to stop me. I felt a surge of pride and relief—my boldness had worked.

But just as I stepped out of the room, I heard a laugh behind me. It was sharp, loud, and mocking. I froze. Something was wrong.

I looked down at the ring in my hand.

It wasn't the special steel ring meant for the device in the doctor's office—it was just an ordinary gold ring.

She had tricked me. She had given me the wrong one. And by taking it, I had revealed that I wasn't who I claimed to be.

There was nothing left to do but leave—defeated and humiliated.

I didn't feel love for her anymore—not the deep, strong kind I might've once had—but I still felt fear, sadness, and a bit of sympathy. I felt it for her, for him, and maybe even for myself. When she finally told me the truth, I felt a strange kind of relief. At least now I understood what I was facing. I laughed, caught up in the pressure of the moment and the sudden sense of clarity.

"Ridiculous," I said. "I know where Madame lives. If I tell the Baltimore police, that man will be just as safe as you or me. Just let me talk to the chief for five minutes and—"

She stopped me with a hand on my arm and a look that made me go quiet.

"What could you do without me?" she said. "And I can't testify. The one thing that would make people believe me—I can't ever say it out loud. I've been part of things that ended people's lives. If I tell the truth, I'll be in serious trouble. I'm not ready to face the law."

That changed everything I thought about her. I took a step back, stunned.

"You've..." I started.

"I've placed that ring on the hand in Dr. Merriam's office three times."

"And each time?"

"Someone in this country died. I don't know how it happened or who did it. But they died."

This woman—so beautiful—had been part of something that awful? I tried not to let my horror show.

"So now it's come to this," I said quietly. "It's either you or him. One of you has to die. You can't both be saved."

She pulled back, pale and shaken. She stared at me for a long time, like she was realizing just how heavy that decision was. In that moment, I felt like I could really see inside her. I saw the blind loyalty that had shut out all reason. I saw anger, confusion, and misguided beliefs—but also, deep down, I saw something good. A spark of honesty and strength that grew brighter and brighter as I watched. Then, with sudden confidence, she spoke.

"You're right," she said. "There's no doubt anymore. I know what I have to do. I'm not worth even one hair on his head. Save him. I'll help you in any way I can."

I didn't wait another second.

"Tell me his name," I said.

She answered quietly, like she was sharing a secret.

I was shocked. I could barely believe it.

"That's unbelievable!" I shouted. "Why would they target him?"

"He's being watched," she said. "That's all it takes."

"This is crazy," I said. "Is this really where things are now?"

"Please," she said, her voice tight with emotion. "No more talking. Don't think—just do something."

"I will," I said, and I ran out of the room.

As I passed her door, I saw her fall into a chair. She looked pale and exhausted, like all her strength was gone. But I didn't stop to help. I knew she wouldn't want me to.

I went straight to the police. My story sounded strange—even to me—and I wasn't exactly calm or clear, since I was trying to protect Miss Calhoun. Still, I eventually got their attention. They sent an officer with me, and I led him to Madame's house.

But when we arrived, I got a shock.

The brass nameplate I remembered was gone. And after we searched a bit, we found out Madame was gone too. She had disappeared—without leaving any clue.

It felt serious. We hurried straight to Dr. Merriam's office.

We knocked on the usual door. No answer.

Then we tried the other door—the one the patients used to exit—and found the doctor himself standing there.

He looked calm and friendly. He said we were there outside of office hours, but still welcomed us in and asked what he could do for us.

I stared at him, surprised. Had he really forgotten me?

He noticed and gave a small smile.

"Oh, I remember you now," he said. "You came earlier today, asking about your friend's strange illness. Do you have more questions? I only have five minutes."

"Please listen to this man first," I said, motioning to the officer.

The doctor politely nodded and turned to the officer, waiting quietly.

The officer didn't waste any time.

"There's a box in your front room that I need to check," he said. "I'm Detective Hopkins from the city police."

Dr. Merriam responded gently, like it was no big deal.

"I'm sorry," he said, "but you're too late."

Then he opened the door to the next room and pointed to the table.

The box was gone.

V.

Doctor Merriam

The second disappointment hit me hard. I couldn't hold back anymore. I turned to the doctor, angry and frustrated, and said sharply:

"Who took the box? Describe them right now. Tell me everything you know about it!"

I didn't even finish my threat, but the look on my face must've been intense, because the doctor stepped back a little and gave the officer a nervous glance before answering.

"So, you don't really have a sick friend, do you?" he said. "Well, well. I gave you some good medical advice anyway. But you paid for it, so we're even."

"The box!" I said again. "The box! Don't waste time—someone's life is in danger!"

He looked surprised, and whether it was fake or real, I couldn't tell.

"You're not making much sense," he said calmly. "A man's life? That's hard to believe."

"But you're not answering me," I said, pushing him for the truth.

He smiled, clearly thinking I was losing my mind.

"That's true," he admitted. "But honestly, I don't know much. I don't know what was inside that box you're so worked up about. I don't even know the names of the people who owned it. It was brought here about six months ago and placed where you saw it earlier today. I agreed to keep it there under certain conditions that worked fine for me and didn't bother my patients. It stayed there until today, when—"

The officer cut in.

"What were the conditions? This is serious. Be honest."

The doctor didn't seem bothered at all.

"The conditions were simple," he said. "The box would stay on the big table by the window for as long as they wanted. Even though it was in my room, it still belonged to their group, so only their members could look at it. I would know who they were because they could open the box. As long as they came during my regular office hours, no one was allowed to question them or interfere. In return, they paid me five dollars a day, through the mail."

"Sounds like a nice deal. And you don't know the names of these people?" the officer asked.

"No," said the doctor. "The first guy who brought it in was short and stocky, with an average face but really sharp eyes. He made all the arrangements. But the man who picked it up and paid me twenty dollars to open the office outside of regular hours—he was different. More polished. He had a thick brown mustache and a serious look. He came with—"

"Why'd you stop?" the officer asked.

The doctor smiled slightly.

"I was deciding whether to say he was with or followed a woman. She was enormous—so large she could barely fit through the doorway. At first I thought she was a patient, since she was brought in sitting in a chair carried by four men. But no, she was only here for the box."

"Madame!" I whispered. And realizing she was directly involved in taking the box, I asked quickly if she had touched it or if it had been removed without being opened.

The doctor's answer crushed the last bit of hope I had.

"She didn't just touch it—she opened it. I saw the lid lift and heard a whirring sound. What's the matter, sir?"

"Nothing," I said quickly. "Nothing I can explain right now. That woman has to be tracked," I told the officer and started to rush out again, when something on the table caught my eye.

"Look!" I said, pointing. A thin wire stuck out from a tiny hole in the middle of the table. "This box was connected to something outside this room."

The doctor's face turned red, and for the first time, he looked a little embarrassed.

"I see that now," he said. "Looks like the person who installed the box did a little extra work while I was out. I wasn't paid for that."

"Where does this wire go?" asked the officer.

"Rip up the floor and find out," the doctor replied. "That's the only way to know."

"But we don't have time for that," I said, hurrying off again—but I stopped once more. "Doctor," I said, "when you agreed to keep this box here under such strange conditions and got paid so well for doing almost nothing, didn't you wonder what it was really being used for? What did you think it was?"

"To be honest," he replied, "I thought it was part of some new kind of lottery scheme. And I still don't know if I was wrong."

I gave him a look but didn't bother correcting him. There was no time.

VI.

The Box Again

There was only one thing left to do—warn Mr. S——— — that he was in danger. But that was easier said than done. If I wanted him to believe me, I'd have to bring up Miss Calhoun. Since he had a strong sense of respect for women, this would make things complicated. It might even stop me from telling him at all. Still, I decided I had to try, even though I wished I were older or had some kind of reputation that would help him take me seriously.

I knew plenty about Mr. S———'s public life, but not much about his personal one—except that he was a widower with one child. I didn't even know where he lived. But the police were able to help, and within thirty minutes of leaving the doctor's office, I was standing in front of his house.

It was a big, old-fashioned home that looked cozy and welcoming. Almost too cozy, considering the dark message I was bringing. The open windows and sunny atmosphere didn't match the warning I carried. How could I talk about something so terrible in a place that felt so peaceful? I figured no one would believe me—but I had to try anyway.

I rang the bell and asked for Mr. S———. He wasn't home. That was my first obstacle. When would he return? The answer gave me some hope—he'd be back by eight. He was throwing a party that evening, and many guests had been invited. That was all the information I could get.

I hurried back to Miss Calhoun and told her everything. I explained how important it was for me to speak to him that night. She looked at me like she was lost in thought. I had to repeat myself twice before she seemed to understand. Then she quickly walked to a desk in the corner and handed me an envelope. It was an invitation to the party—one she had received a week ago.

"I'll get you one too," she whispered. "But don't talk to him right away. Don't say anything unless I'm nearby and you signal me first. I'll be close. I think I'll be strong enough to face this moment."

"God willing, your sacrifice will make a difference," I told her, and then I left.

It was tough walking into a house full of music, flowers, lights, and laughter—especially with the heavy truth I carried. But knowing how serious this was—for both me and for the woman I had nearly fallen in love with—I felt a strange calm inside me. The kind of calm people sometimes feel when facing something big. I checked my reflection before leaving the dressing room to make sure I looked normal—not too pale, not too red—then stepped into the crowd, looking for Mr. S———.

I expected him to be good-looking, but not quite like he was. There was a sadness in his expression, mixed with quiet strength. Nobody else in the room had his presence. He looked like he was trying to enjoy the party, but you could still see the weight he carried. I wondered—had someone already warned him? Or was this just how he normally looked?

I didn't know, so I focused on my task. I pushed through the crowd, hoping for a chance to speak to him alone. At the same time, I spotted two detectives from the police. They were standing near the doorway, blending in with the guests.

Whether he meant to or not, Mr. S——— had placed himself near the conservatory. As I got closer, I spotted Miss Calhoun standing among the plants. She caught my eye and gave me a quick, subtle signal. I remembered what she had asked.

I quietly left the group I was in and circled toward the side door she had motioned to. A moment later, I was standing next to her. She was wearing a velvet gown that made her skin look almost like stone.

"He knows something," she said. "He's not clueless like we thought. I've been watching him for an hour. He's expecting something. That might help us."

"You didn't tell him anything?" I asked.

"No. I couldn't."

"Maybe the detectives said something."

"Maybe. But they don't know everything."

"No, they can't. That's why we still need to speak with him."

"Mr. Abbott," she said quickly, her voice shaky and rushed, "don't go to him yet. Let me calm down first. I just need a few minutes. But wait—what if waiting is too dangerous? What if it costs him his life? No—go now, go right now. Just—"

She suddenly stopped, stumbled back, and fell into a chair beneath a large plant.

"He's coming. Please don't leave me, Mr. Abbott. Stay nearby, behind those plants. I can't face him alone."

I did what she asked. Mr. S—— walked in with a smile on his face—the first one I'd seen—and walked straight to Miss Calhoun. She tried to stand, but couldn't. He seemed pleased by that.

"Irene," he said, and the sound of his voice made me regret hiding. "I thought I saw you come in here. Now that all the guests are here, I snuck away for a moment. I couldn't wait any longer. Irene, you look pale. You're shaking. Did I scare you? Maybe I was too direct. We've always kept a certain distance... but didn't you know how I felt? Didn't you know I loved you? Ever since I met you, all I've wanted was to make you my wife."

"Oh my God..." I saw her mouth the words, though no sound came out. She looked completely stunned—overwhelmed and lit up at the same time.

"Mr. S——," she said, trying her best to speak calmly, "I didn't expect this. I never imagined you'd say that. I don't deserve this. I'm not worthy of such love. I shouldn't even be hearing these words. Besides—"

She couldn't finish. Or maybe he wouldn't let her.

"Not worthy? You?" His voice was full of emotion. "Then what do you think of me? I want you to marry me because you're better than I'll ever be. I need someone kind, someone good, someone pure."

"Mr. S———," she said, standing now, her face full of strength and glowing with emotion, "I'm not the woman you think I am. I'm not pure—not in thought or action. I've been involved in things most women couldn't even imagine. I'm part of a group—yes, I regret it—but it's a group that ignores what's right and puts selfish goals above everything else. And—"

He gently bent down and kissed her hand.

"You don't have to say anything else," he whispered. "I understand. But... will you still marry me?"

She stared at him, frozen with shock. Her face was pale, and her eyes were wide with fear.

"Understand? You understand? What are you talking about? Why would you understand?"

"Because," he said so quietly it was almost a breath—but I heard every word—"because I'm the leader of the group you were talking about. Irene... now you know my secret."

She didn't say a word, but her silence was full of pain. I think he felt it too, because his expression suddenly turned soft and full of sadness.

"I know this is hard," he said. "I don't blame you. It's a terrible truth—I've started to see that myself. That's why I let myself fall in love. I needed something good to escape from all this. But now, knowing how good and honest you really are... it just makes the truth harder to ignore. Still, this isn't the right time or place to talk about all of that. Please, try to smile, my dear, and—"

"Wait!" she said, finally finding her strength. She grabbed his arm. "Did you know someone was sentenced today?"

His face darkened. "Yes," he said, nodding and glancing toward the party. "I heard the bell while I was out. I didn't know someone's name had already been chosen."

She sank down into a seat and covered her face with her hands. I think she was trying not to scream. But then she pulled her hands away, leaned close to him, and whispered quickly:

"You're the leader and you didn't know? These people—they're going behind your back! They're jealous of your power!"

He looked shocked. He glanced at the door, then turned to her as if he was going to ask a question—but she didn't give him time.

"Do you even know who the bell rang for today?" she asked.

He shook his head. "No. I'm waiting for someone to bring me the name," he said, glancing toward the back of the conservatory. "Is it someone at the party?"

Her gasp was so loud it could've reached the next room. She looked like she couldn't breathe or speak. I almost stepped forward to help, but just then, I heard a soft click from the back door.

I looked—and saw the strange man from Madame's place. The one with the sloped forehead. He was pushing through the plants… holding the box.

I froze, sinking deeper into my hiding spot. But Mr. S—— seemed almost relieved.

"Ah, he's here!" he said, and walked quickly to the drawing-room door, locked it, took the key, and returned to meet the man.

The man looked thrilled in a creepy, awful way. His lips were pressed tightly together, and his pale face looked twisted with excitement. He moved slowly, like something cold and sneaky that knew its target couldn't get away.

Watching him, I felt like both my life and Mr. S——'s could end any second. I stayed still, barely breathing. Miss Calhoun let out a long, shaky sigh. The man heard it, bowed slightly, but kept his eyes locked on Mr. S——.

"I was told to give you this box—no matter where you were or who you were with. The name is inside."

Mr. S—— looked at the box, then at the man, his face filled with anger and confusion.

"This isn't how we do things," he said. "Why wasn't I told that a name was being considered? And why did you take the box from its place? You broke the connection we worked so hard to set up."

As he spoke, he glanced through the glass walls of the conservatory toward a tall building at the end of the garden—the same building where I had first seen the box. Now I finally understood how the two places had been secretly linked.

Mr. S—— looked up without meaning to. Then he dropped his gaze, gave a slight nod, and said, "You can speak in front of her. She has a key."

"The connection was cut because someone got suspicious," the man explained. "As for your other question—the answer is inside the box. Want me to open it?"

Mr. S—— frowned, shook his head, and pulled a key from his pocket. Then he turned to Miss Calhoun.

"Do you understand what this means?" he asked.

She didn't answer with words—just pointed to the box.

Her expression said: Open it.

Mr. S—— unlocked the box and lifted the lid.

"Look under the hand," the man instructed.

Mr. S—— leaned over the small table where the box sat, reached beneath the metal hand, and pulled out a folded piece of paper. As he read it, the color drained from his face.

"How many people agreed to this?" he asked.

"You'll notice the hand has five rings," the man replied.

Miss Calhoun flinched and opened her mouth like she was about to speak—but stayed quiet when she saw Mr. S—— unfold the paper.

"The name of the newest traitor," the man said in a cold voice, his expression full of hatred like I'd never seen before.

But Mr. S—— and Miss Calhoun didn't see the hate on his face. Mr. S—— just stared at the paper, shocked. She kept her eyes on him, clearly worried. Meanwhile, cheerful music from the party drifted in from the other room.

Then we heard a soft crinkle.

Mr. S—— had crushed the paper in his hand.

"So," he said, finally locking eyes with the man, "the group has decided I'm the one who must die. Now I understand how the others felt—the ones who were sentenced before me without a chance to defend themselves. But you won't be the one to kill me. If I'm going to die, it'll be by someone else."

He leaned in and whispered something into the messenger's ear. I couldn't hear it, but whatever it was, it clearly disappointed the man. His shoulders sagged, and he gave Mr. S—— a bitter, sideways look that made me shiver. Still, he didn't leave right away.

"Tonight?" he asked.

"Tonight," Mr. S—— repeated, pointing to the door the man had come through. When he still hesitated, Mr. S—— grabbed his arm and firmly led him through the conservatory, whispering, "Go. I'm still the chief."

The man gave a small bow and slowly walked out into the night.

Music and laughter echoed from the other room.

Mr. S—— and Miss Calhoun stood silently, facing each other.

"You should go home," he said softly. Then, his voice full of pain, he added, "Was I really such a bad leader that even you thought I was holding back the group's mission?"

His words struck a nerve in her.

"No!" she cried. "This is all a lie. A setup! Didn't you get the letter I sent this morning? The one addressed to the chief, written the usual way?"

"No," he replied.

"Then someone betrayed you even worse than you thought. I wrote to say my ring had been stolen—that I didn't agree with the decision to sentence the man they were watching. I warned that if they used my name, it would be fake. I sent it before I knew the man in danger was you. Now—"

"Now what?"

"Now you need to go after the woman called Madame. That messenger you just sent away—he'd forgive you for turning him down if you let him go after someone even worse: her. She pretends to predict death, but she's the one making sure people die."

"Irene—"

But she couldn't stop. Everything came spilling out. She told him everything that had happened over the last day. She was clearly hoping he'd find comfort in it—or maybe hope.

But he didn't. And his next words explained why.

"Madame may be dangerous," he said, "but she's just one of five leaders. The other three are smart, honest men. They might believe I've failed as a leader. And maybe they're right. I've started to doubt everything. If they've truly lost faith in me, then neither Madame's hate nor your love can stop what's coming. I can't let other people face the group's justice and then run from it myself. If I did, I wouldn't deserve your love. And right now, your love means more to me than anything."

She hadn't expected that. She hadn't realized how strong he really was. But of course, without that strength, he could never have led the group for so long.

"But the vote wasn't fair," she said. "It broke the rules. You need five honest votes, and only four were real. If you let them get away with this, you're helping them cheat. And I know you're better than that."

But even that didn't make him change his mind.

"I see five rings," he said. "And I see something else, too. Even if I wanted to take the way out you're offering, they'd never really let me live. Once a leader shows fear, his people stop trusting him. I'd still be killed—maybe right away, maybe in some horrible way—and probably when I'm not ready. And you, Irene, my strong and beautiful love... they wouldn't spare you either."

He paused before going on. "And don't forget the young man who helped you—he risked everything to try to save me. If I ruin Madame's plan, what do you think will happen to him? Nothing could protect him. I've been responsible for the deaths of others. Now it's my turn to face what I've done."

He looked at her, his voice calm but steady. "Kiss me, Irene... and leave. That's an order—from your chief."

She let out a soft, heartbroken sound and gave in. She lifted her face, gave him a kiss filled with deep sadness, and slowly walked out through the door into the garden. As the door closed behind her, he sighed deeply, like he was saying goodbye to life. Then, just a moment later, he lifted his head, straightened his shoulders, and walked right into the middle of the party—smiling, joking, and laughing like nothing had happened.

No one noticed when I quietly left. By the next morning, I was in Philadelphia. That's where I read the news:

"Baltimore, Md.—A sudden tragedy took place last night. Mr. S——, a respected businessman and political leader, collapsed and died during a dinner toast in front of a hundred guests. His death is a major loss for the Southern cause. The city is mourning."

Later in the paper, in a small corner, I found this short line:

"Baltimore, Md.—A young woman named Irene Calhoun was found dead this morning. Officials believe she took poison. No one knows why."

The End

Thank You for Reading

Dear Reader,

We hope this timeless classic has sparked your imagination and enriched your literary journey. Now that you've turned the final page, we want to share a vision for the future of reading—one where every classic you've ever wanted to explore is at your fingertips, in a format that best suits your life.

We'd like to invite you to gain immediate, unlimited digital & audiobook access to hundreds of the most treasured literary classics ever written—along with the option to secure deluxe paperback, hardcover & box set editions at printing cost. Together, we can spark a new global literary renaissance alongside our small, independent publishing house called "The Library of Alexandria."

Thousands of years ago, the Library of Alexandria stood as a beacon of knowledge—until it was lost to history. We aim to reignite that spirit of preservation and discovery right now, in the modern age—only this time, it's accessible to all, in every language and every format.

Picture a world where every timeless classic, novel, poem, or philosophical treatise is not only available to read but also updated for today's readers—modernized, translated into any language or dialect, and ready to enjoy in any format you choose, whether that is in an eBook, audiobook, paperback, or deluxe hardcover & box set version a printing cost.

By joining our movement to rebuild the modern Library of Alexandria, you become part of an unprecedented mission to offer:

- **Unlimited Audiobook & eBook Access to the Greatest Classics of All Time**

  Instantly explore thousands of legendary works, from Plato and Shakespeare to Jane Austen and Leo Tolstoy. All are instantly ready to read or listen to, giving you a complete literary universe at your fingertips.

- **Paperback & Deluxe Editions at Printing Costs:**

  Purchase any title in a paperback, deluxe hardbound, or deluxe boxset edition at printing costs, shipped right to your doorstep. Curate your personal library of Alexandria with editions worthy of display— crafted to last, designed to captivate, and delivered straight to your door.

- **Modern translations for Contemporary Readers in all languages and dialects**

  Discover a vast selection of classics reimagined in clear, current language—no more struggling with outdated phrases or obscure references. Next to the original versions, we aim to offer translations in as many languages and dialects as possible.

  As we continue our translation efforts and add new languages, readers everywhere can connect with these works as if they were written today. By bridging linguistic divides, you're contributing to ensuring that these timeless stories become more meaningful, accessible, and inspiring for people across the globe.

- **Your Personal Library of Alexandria:**

  Over the months and years, you'll curate a unique physical archive of classics—each volume a testament to your taste, curiosity, and love of knowledge. It's not just about owning books—it's about curating a cultural legacy you'll cherish and pass down for generations to come.

- **Join a Global Literary Renaissance:**

  Your support fuels an ongoing mission: allowing us to reinvest in offering deluxe print editions (including special boxsets) at their true cost, broaden the range of available formats and translations, and extend the reach of these works to new audiences worldwide. By joining today, you're not just preserving a legacy of masterpieces; you set in motion a powerful wave of literary accessibility.

We are more than a publisher—we're a movement, and we can't do it alone. Your support lets us scale our mission, preserving and reimagining history's greatest works for tomorrow's readers.

Become a Torchbearer of knowledge.

Thank you for picking up this book and allowing us into your literary journey. As you turn the pages, know that you're part of something larger: a global effort to keep these stories alive, share their wisdom across borders and generations, and spark a true cultural revival for the modern era.

If this resonates with you—please consider taking the next step by visiting:

www.libraryofalexandria.com

With gratitude and a shared love of knowledge,

The Modern Library of Alexandria Team

Visit:

www.libraryofalexandria.com

Or scan the code below:

www.ingramcontent.com/pod-product-compliance
Lightning Source LLC
Chambersburg PA
CBHW011525240626
47154CB00009B/2970